BOY OF THEIR DREAMS

By Eleanor Robins

Development: Kent Publishing Services, Inc.
Design and Production: Signature Design Group, Inc.
Illustrations: Jan Naimo Jones

SADDLEBACK PUBLISHING, INC.
Three Watson
Irvine, CA 92618-2767

E-Mail: info@sdlback.com
Website: www.sdlback.com

ISBN 1-56254-679-1

Printed in th

1 2 3 4 5 6

Chapter 1

It was the first day of school. Kim was in math class. She had Mr. Wong for math. It was time for class to start.

A boy came in. Kim had never seen him before. He must be new at the school.

There was also a new girl in the class. She was sitting in front of Kim.

The boy went over to Mr. Wong.

The new girl turned around. She said, "Hi. I guess it is OK to talk for a few minutes. My name is Gail. I'm new here."

Kim wanted to keep looking at the new boy. But she didn't want to be rude.

Kim said, "My name is Kim. Glad you are here at our school. I hope you like it here."

Gail said, "Thanks. I hope I will too. But I am not so sure I will."

That surprised Kim.

"Why?" Kim asked.

It was just the first day of school. So why did Gail think she might not like it?

Gail said, "I did OK at my other school. But I am not sure I will here. This is a big school. And I don't know the teachers."

"Most of them are OK," Kim said.

"What about Mr. Wong?" Gail asked.

Kim said, "He is OK. He is a hard teacher. But kids learn a lot from him."

Gail said, "Thanks for telling me.

I hope I am in some more of your classes."

Just then Mr. Wong said, "Time to start class. Open your books. We have a lot to do this semester."

Kim didn't see where the new boy went. He must be sitting in the back of the class. She wanted to turn around and look for him. But she didn't.

Kim opened her math book. But she was thinking about the new boy. He was not that cute. But there was something about him that she liked.

She kept thinking about him. And she had to try hard to keep her mind on math.

She was glad when class was over. She was going to look for him. She hoped he would be in some more of her classes.

Gail turned around. She said, "Can

I call you about this homework? I am not sure I know how to do it."

"Sure," Kim said.

She gave her phone number to Gail.

Gail said, "Thanks, Kim. I might call you after school."

Kim got up and looked for the new boy. But she did not see him. He must have left when Gail was talking to her.

Gail said, "What class do you have next? Maybe we have the same class."

"Science with Mr. Reese," Kim said.

"I don't have science next," Gail said.

Kim was in a hurry to go. She said, "Call me after school about the math."

Then she hurried out into the hall.

Fran walked up to her. Kim didn't think she would see Fran until lunch. So she was surprised to see Fran.

Fran was her best friend. They had been best friends since third grade. Fran had been there for her in good times. And in bad times like when her mom and dad split up.

Fran had a big smile on her face.

Fran said, "It is about time. I thought you would never get out of that class."

Kim said, "Sorry. I didn't know you were going to meet me after class."

"That's OK. But I wanted to talk to you," Fran said.

"About what?" Kim asked.

"I can't tell you now. Or I will be late to class. I will have to tell you at lunch. See you then. Don't be late," Fran said.

Fran hurried down the hall.

Kim wanted to know what Fran had to tell her. And she wished she had left class sooner.

Kim turned to go to her locker. She saw the new boy. He was looking at her.

Kim smiled at him.

He smiled back at her.

Chapter 2

Kim got her science book out of her locker. Then she hurried to her science class. She got there just as the bell rang.

Kim looked for the new boy. But she didn't see him.

She sat down in front of Griff. He had been in some of her classes last year.

Mr. Reese called the roll. Then he said, "Today we will start on Chapter 1. We will read most of it in class. You need to read the rest at home. You will have a test on it next week."

"Just great. Only the first day. And he is talking about a test," said Griff so only Kim could hear him.

Kim tried to keep her mind on science. But she kept thinking about the new boy. When would she see him again? Did he like her too? Or did he smile at her only because she smiled at him?

Kim liked science OK. But she was glad when class was over.

Griff said, "See you tomorrow. Unless I can get out of this class."

Kim said, "Why try? You have to take science from someone."

"Yeah. I know," Griff said.

But Kim knew he did not like to study.

It was time for Kim to go to lunch. She wished she didn't have lunch so early.

But she could hardly wait to see Fran. She wanted to know what Fran had to tell her. She also wanted to tell Fran about the new boy. She wished she knew his name.

Kim quickly left class and went to her locker. She put away her books. Then she hurried to the lunch room.

Fran was at a table. She waved at Kim. She had a big smile on her face.

Kim quickly got her lunch. She went to the table and sat down.

"I thought you would never get here," Fran said.

"Why? What's going on?" Kim asked.

Fran said, "I have a new boy in my math class. He is so cute. And he sits next to me."

So that was why Fran looked so happy.

"His name is Clay. He is on the football team. And he is so cute," Fran said.

Fran didn't give Kim time to talk.

"And he said he would help me with math. He is so cute, Kim," Fran said.

Kim laughed. She said, "I know. You have told me three times that he is."

Fran laughed. She said, "Sorry. But he is cute."

So was the boy in Kim's class. But he was not that cute.

Kim said, "Do you think Clay will ask you out?"

Fran said, "I sure hope so. I told him I didn't have a boyfriend."

That surprised Kim. She said, "You did?"

Fran didn't have a boyfriend. But why did she tell the new boy that? She had just met him.

Fran said, "Yes. I told him that was why I needed help in math. That I didn't have a boyfriend to help me."

"Why did you tell him that? You have always done OK in math," Kim said.

Fran said, "I know. But I might need some help this year."

Then Fran laughed.

Kim said, "I get it now. You hope he will help you with math. And then ask you for a date. Since he knows you don't have a boyfriend."

"Right," Fran said.

Kim hoped he would ask Fran for a date.

Fran said, "Now your turn. How was your morning? Any new boys in your classes?"

"Yes. One," Kim said.

"Is he cute?" Fran asked.

Kim said, "Kind of. But not real cute. But there is something about him that I really like."

"Tell me more," Fran said.

Kim said, "There is not a lot more to

tell. But he did smile at me."

"Great. He must like you too," Fran said.

Kim said, "I don't know. I smiled at him first. So that may be why he smiled at me."

"It doesn't matter. He still smiled at you. Is he on the football team? I hope he is," Fran said.

"I don't know. I don't know much about him. Just that he is new. And he is in my math class," Kim said.

"You didn't find out his name?" Fran said.

Kim said, "No. He was late to class. And then I didn't see him when class was over."

"Clay was late to my class. Very late. But I sure am glad he got there," Fran said.

Kim looked at her watch.

"Lunch time will be over soon. We need to stop talking and eat," Kim said.

Fran said, "OK. I need to hurry. Clay may be in my next class. I sure hope so. And I want to sit next to him."

Kim hoped the new boy would be in her next class too.

Chapter 3

But the new boy was not in Kim's next class.

She saw Fran when the class was over. They were in the hall at the same time.

"Clay was in my science class too. And I got to sit next to him," Fran said.

Kim was glad he was in Fran's class.

"Was the new boy in your class?" Fran asked.

"No," Kim said.

Fran said, "Too bad. Do you have volleyball practice after school today?"

Kim was on the volleyball team. But Fran wasn't.

Kim said, "No. We don't have a game this week. So we are going to practice only three days. And practice longer those days."

"Good. What do you have to do right after school?" Fran said.

"I have to study. But not right after school," Kim said.

"Good. I have a great idea," Fran said.

"What?" Kim asked.

Kim was always glad to hear a great idea.

"We can go down to the football field. And watch the boys practice," Fran said.

"Is that a joke? Why would we want to do that?" Kim asked.

She could think of a lot of things more fun than that. It might even be more fun to study.

Fran didn't look happy. She said, "I thought you liked football."

Kim said, "I like football games. But that is not the same as practice."

Fran said, "I know that. But I told you. He is on the team."

"Who?" Kim asked.

"Clay," Fran said.

"Oh," Kim said. She had forgot the cute new boy was on the team.

"Will you go? For me?" Fran said.

"OK. Just for you," Kim said.

Fran said, "Thanks, Kim."

After school the girls went down to the football field. The players were already there.

Kim and Fran went over to the stands and sat down. Some other girls were there too. And some boys.

Fran said, "I see him. I see him."

"Which one is he?" Kim asked.

They were too far away for Kim to see who the players were. So how did Fran know?

Fran told Kim his number.

"How do you know that is his number?" Kim asked.

"I asked him after science," Fran said.

Kim looked at the boys run up and down the field. She saw them pass the ball. And she saw them tackle.

Kim could hardly wait to go.

"Isn't this fun?" Fran said.

"Sure. Lots of fun," Kim said.

It would not be long until they left. So why tell Fran it wasn't fun to her?

She wished the new boy in her class played ball. Then it might be fun for her too.

Chapter 4

It was the next morning. Kim could hardly wait to get to math class. She got there early to see the new boy.

But he did not come to class. Was he absent? On just the second day of school?

Gail was there. She said, "Can you look at my homework? And make sure I did it right."

"Sure," Kim said.

Kim looked at Gail's homework.

Then Kim said, "It looks right to me."

"Thanks. I thought it was. But I wasn't sure," Gail said.

Mr. Wong said, "Time to start class. Get out your homework."

Kim had to try hard to keep her mind on math. Where was the new boy?

She was glad when math class was over.

Gail said, "See you tomorrow, Kim."

"OK. Have a good day," Kim said.

She got her books and hurried into the hall.

She saw the new boy. Why wasn't he in her math class? Was he late to school?

He walked over to Kim. He said, "I saw you and your friend at practice. Thanks for being there."

Kim got pushed on down the hall. So she didn't get to say anything back to him.

He was on the football team too.

She wished she knew his number. And his name.

She went to science class and sat down. Griff was already there.

Griff said, "No luck. I can't drop this class. And they won't let me have another teacher. I need your phone number. I might have to call you for some help."

Kim gave him her number. But she wasn't sure she wanted him to have it.

Did he want it just to call her about science? Or was he going to ask her for a date?

Just then Mr. Reese started class. He called on Kim three times. And she had to try hard to keep her mind on science.

She kept thinking about the new boy.

She was glad when class was over. She hurried into the hall.

Griff said, "Kim, wait up."

Kim stopped. She hoped he wasn't going to ask her for a date.

"What pages do we have to read for homework?" Griff asked.

Kim told him.

She saw the new boy. He was looking at her and Griff. She didn't want him to think she dated Griff.

She smiled and waved at him. He waved back. Then he went on down the hall.

Kim wished she could have talked to him.

She hurried to the lunch room. She could hardly wait to see Fran.

They both got their food quickly and sat down.

Kim said, "He is on the football team too."

She didn't have to tell Fran who he was. Fran would know.

"Great. How did you find out?" Fran said.

"He saw us at practice. And he thanked me for being there," Kim said.

Fran said, "He did. That is just great. He must like you a lot."

Kim thought he might too. But she was not sure. Maybe he was just being nice.

"Did he say anything else to you? Like his name?" Fran asked.

Kim said, "No. I just saw him in the hall after math. He didn't come to math class. I saw him after science too. But Griff was talking to me. I hope he doesn't think I date Griff."

Fran said, "Clay was in my class. I talked to him. He didn't say he saw me at practice. He must not have seen us. I wish we could go back today. But you have volleyball practice."

"You can go," Kim said.

Fran said, "I know. But I don't want to go by myself."

Kim wished she could go with Fran. But she was glad she had volleyball practice. She liked volleyball. She just wished she was on the starting team.

"Do you have practice tomorrow?" Fran asked.

"Yes," Kim said.

"What about Thursday?" Fran asked.

"No," Kim said.

Fran said, "Good. Maybe we can go watch the football team then."

"OK," Kim said.

Maybe by then she would know the number of the new boy.

Chapter 5

It was the next day. Kim hurried to the lunch room. She had not seen the new boy all morning.

Was he at school?

Fran was at a table. She waved her hands for Kim to hurry. Kim quickly got her food and sat down.

"What's going on, Fran?" Kim asked.

Fran said, "Clay did see us at practice. He said he looked for us yesterday."

Kim knew that made Fran very happy.

"And he asked me when we have lunch. He has lunch now too. He said he would try to come by our table. And say hello," Fran said.

"Great, Fran," Kim said.

She was happy for Fran. Maybe Clay liked Fran as much as Fran liked him.

"Did you see your new boy?" Fran asked.

"No," Kim said.

"Maybe you will see him after lunch. Let's hurry and eat. In case Clay does come by," Fran said.

The girls ate and did not talk.

After a few minutes Fran got a big smile on her face.

Fran said, "There he is. He saw us. And he is on his way over here." Fran looked very happy.

Kim wanted to turn around and look. But she didn't.

Then a boy said, "Hi, Fran. OK for me to sit with you for a few minutes?"

“Sure,” Fran said.

Kim thought she had heard the boy’s voice before. But she had to be wrong. She just had to be.

Then Kim saw him. Oh, no. She was not wrong. Clay was the new boy in her math class.

But how could he be in two classes at the same time?

But then Kim knew. He was in the wrong class the first day. He left when she was talking with Gail. That was why she didn’t see him at the end of the class. And why he had not been back.

Clay sat down at the table.

Fran said, “Clay, this is my friend Kim. Kim, this is Clay.”

Clay gave Kim a big smile. He said, “Hi, Kim. I am glad to meet you at last. Fran has said a lot of nice things about you.”

“Thanks,” Kim made herself say.

How could she have been so wrong? She thought he liked her. But he knew she was Fran’s friend. That was why he had talked to her.

“Thanks for coming to practice,” he said to both of them.

Fran said, "It was fun. I just love football. So does Kim. I hope we can both go to the game next week."

Kim knew why Fran said that. Fran hoped Clay would ask her to be his date after the game. And that the boy in Kim's math class would ask her.

But Fran didn't know they were the same boy. And she didn't want Fran to know.

Fran talked on about how she loved football. And about how she hoped to see the game next week.

Kim had to get away from the two of them. She was sure it would be OK with Fran for her to go. She was sure Fran would like to be alone with Clay. Then maybe he would ask her for a date.

Kim stood up.

"Don't go," Clay said.

Fran said, "You don't have to go, Kim. Stay and talk to us."

But Kim knew that Fran didn't want her to stay. And she had to get away from them.

Kim said, "I can't. I need to look over some notes before my next class."

But she didn't have to look over any notes.

She had been so sure that Clay liked her. How could she have been so wrong?

She was very glad she had volleyball practice after school. So she wouldn't have to talk to Fran about Clay.

Chapter 6

Kim was at her locker the next morning.

She saw Clay. He was walking down the hall. She quickly looked the other way. She didn't want to talk to him. She hoped he didn't see her.

Kim got her science book. She started to go to class.

"Kim, wait," Clay called to her.

At first Kim didn't stop. She acted like she did not hear him.

"Kim, wait," Clay called again.

Kim stopped. She didn't want Clay to wonder why she didn't wait.

"Do you have a minute?" he asked.

"Only a minute," Kim said.

What did he want? It must be something about Fran.

Clay said, "Then I will ask you quickly. Do you want to go out with me Friday night?"

That surprised Kim very much. She just looked at him. She must not have heard him right.

Clay said, "I know I am asking you late. But I didn't meet you until yesterday. You left the lunch room before I could ask you. Griff gave me your phone number this morning. But I didn't know how to call you last night."

"What about Fran?" Kim asked.

Wasn't Fran the girl he liked?

Clay looked surprised. He said, "Fran can go with us. I will get her a date with a boy on the football team."

Kim could not believe what he was saying.

He liked her and not Fran.

She didn't know what to say to him.

"I can't talk now. I have to go. I can't be late to science," Kim said.

She had to get away from him and think.

"OK. I will call you after school," Clay said.

Kim hurried to science. She was almost late.

Griff said, "You better get a move on it next time. You were almost late."

Kim wished Griff would not talk to her.

All she could think about was Clay. And that he had asked her for a date. There was no way she could keep her mind on science.

Mr. Reese called on her three times. But she didn't even know what he had asked her.

Mr. Reese said, "Kim, keep your mind on science. You will have a test on this next week."

Griff said, "What is wrong with you today? You have to listen. Or you won't be able to help me study."

Griff didn't say it very loudly. Only so Kim could hear him.

Kim liked Griff OK. But she hoped he would find someone else to help him study.

She was glad when science was over. But she didn't want to go to lunch.

What would she say to Fran?

For the first time ever she didn't want to eat lunch with Fran.

Chapter 7

Kim started to walk slowly to lunch.

Fran was her best friend. They told each other everything.

But should she tell Fran that Clay asked her for a date?

Kim got to the lunch room. She didn't want to go in. But she did.

Fran was at a table. She waved at Kim.

Kim slowly got her lunch. She walked slowly to the table and sat down.

Fran said, "Are you OK, Kim? You don't look so good. Are you sick?"

"I didn't do well in science. I am just

thinking about that," Kim said.

Kim didn't do well in science. But that was not what she was thinking about. And that was not what she was upset about.

"Did you have a test?" Fran asked.

"No," Kim said.

Fran said, "Then don't worry about it. Just do well tomorrow."

Kim looked at her lunch. It looked OK. But she did not want to eat.

And there was no way she could watch football practice with Fran.

"I can't go with you to watch football practice today. I need to study," Kim said.

She did need to study. But that wasn't why she didn't want to go.

"Oh, well. Maybe we can go next week," Fran said.

Kim didn't say anything.

Fran said, "What did you think about Clay? Isn't he cute? I wanted to ask you after school yesterday. But you had volleyball practice. And I didn't have time to call you."

Kim was glad. Because she was too upset to talk then. But she was more upset now.

But she had to say something.

"Yes, Clay is cute," Kim said.

She wished Fran would stop talking about Clay. But Fran didn't.

Fran said, "He likes you. He told me he did in math."

"He did?" Kim said.

Fran said "Yes. I asked him how he liked you."

"Why did you ask him that?" Kim asked.

Maybe Fran knew he liked her.

Maybe that was why she asked him. Maybe it would be OK to date him.

Fran said, "I like Clay a lot. And you are my best friend. I want the two of you to like each other."

They liked each other. That was for sure.

Fran said, "Clay helped me with math today. He is so nice. I gave him my phone number."

That surprised Kim. She said, "Did he ask for it?"

Did he plan to date both girls?

Fran said, "No. I just gave it to him. He hasn't asked me for a date in class. So I gave him my number. In case he doesn't like to ask for a date at school. Do you think he will call me tonight?"

Kim did not know what to say.

"Well? What do you think?" Fran asked.

Kim said, "I don't know. You never know about boys."

That was for sure.

Fran said, "I will soon find out. But I have talked too much about me. Now about you. Was the new boy in your class today?"

"No," Kim said.

Kim did not want to talk about him.

"Did you see him in the hall?" Fran asked.

Kim didn't know what to say.

How could she tell Fran that the boy was Clay? And that he had asked her for a date?

Fran liked him so much. Fran had never liked a boy that much before.

"Did you hear me, Kim? Did you see him in the hall?" Fran asked.

Kim had to say something.

But she could not tell Fran. Not yet.

"He may have moved," Kim said.

Kim had never lied to Fran before.

Fran said, "I sure hope not. I know how much you like him. Almost as much as I like Clay."

Kim wanted so much to date Clay. She had never wanted to date a boy that much before. How could she turn down a date with him?

But how could she date Clay? Fran liked him so much too.

Kim needed some time to think about what she was going to do.

Chapter 8

After lunch Kim did try to keep her mind on her work. But she could not do it. All she could think about was Clay. And about what she should do.

She saw Fran after her last class.

Fran said, "I can hardly wait to get home. Clay just has to call. But I know he can't until practice is over."

Kim couldn't tell Fran that Clay said he would call her. And not Fran.

"Wish me luck, Kim," Fran said.

"Good luck, Fran," Kim said.

But Kim could not say she hoped Clay called Fran.

Why did they have to like the same boy?

Kim was glad to get home. She needed more time to think. She was glad she didn't have volleyball practice.

What should she do?

Maybe she should tell Fran. Maybe Fran would tell her it was OK to date Clay. Fran might tell her that. But Kim knew Fran would not mean it. Fran liked Clay too much for it to be OK.

The phone rang. It was too soon for Clay to call. At least Kim hoped it was.

It was Griff.

Kim was glad it was not Clay. She still didn't know what she would say to him.

Kim hoped Griff didn't call to ask her for a date. She had too much to think about now.

But she didn't think Griff had called to ask her out. She didn't think he liked her that way.

"What pages do we have to read?" Griff asked.

Didn't he ever listen in class?

Kim told him the pages they had to read.

Then he hung up. He didn't thank her. Or even tell her good-bye.

What should Kim do?

It would not be long until Clay would call.

Should she tell Clay that she couldn't date him? Then maybe Clay would ask Fran out. But she didn't know he would do that.

She did not want to turn Clay down. Maybe she could date him. Maybe she could work everything out with Fran. And they could stay friends.

The phone rang again.

Kim went to the phone.

It was Gail. Kim was glad it was not Fran. Or Clay.

Gail said, "I need some help with math. Do you have time to help me?"

"Sure," Kim said.

But she didn't really have time to help Gail. She needed time to think.

But it didn't take long for Kim to help Gail.

"Thanks for the help, Kim. My best friend helped me at my other school. I sure do miss her. We did everything together," Gail said.

Just like Kim and Fran did.

Fran had been there to share the good times. And she had been there to help Kim in the bad times.

Kim wanted to keep sharing her good and bad times with Fran.

It was hard to find a best friend. One you could trust. She could trust Fran.

And Fran trusted her too.

She could not hurt Fran. They had been best friends for a long time.

Kim liked Clay a lot. But she would not lose her best friend to date him. She still wanted to date Clay. But she would not give up her friendship with Fran to do it.